MERTHYR
TYDFIL
D1140267

All in a Day's Work

Jenny Alexander

Illustrated by Rhiannon Powell

Merthyr Tydfil Libraries

02545810

Contents

PROPERTY OF MERTHYR
TYDFIL PUBLIC LIBRARIES

A Fire
in Wellington Square

Mr Keeping went to the police station.
'My chimp is missing,' he said.
The policewoman picked up her pen.
'What does he look like?' she asked.
'He looks like... a chimp!' said Mr Keeping.
'Please can you help me find him?'

Just then, PC Kent came in. 'Good morning
Mr Keeping,' he said. 'How is Brian?'
'Brian is missing,' said Mr Keeping.
PC Kent put on his hat.
'I am on my way to Wellington Square,
so I can help you to look for him,' he said.

As they walked to Wellington Square,
PC Kent told Mr Keeping
that he was going to see Mr Patel.
Someone had taken a big box of sweets
from Mr Patel's shop that morning.

PC Kent asked everyone they passed,
'Have you seen a chimp?'
Mr Keeping said, 'When I ask people if they
have seen a chimp they just look at me as if I
am mad. I am glad you are here to help me.'
But nobody had seen Brian.

They went into Mr Patel's shop.
Mr Patel showed PC Kent where
the missing box of sweets had been.

PC Kent asked Mr Patel if he could remember who had been into the shop that morning.

'Here is a list I made for you,' said Mr Patel. 'I told Jamila the names and she wrote them down. She always has a notepad in her pocket.'

Mr Keeping was looking out of the shop window.
He said, 'You should clean your window,
Mr Patel. I can hardly see the park at all.'

PC Kent looked round. He frowned.
He opened the door.
They still could hardly see the park,
because the whole square was full of smoke.

PC Kent called the fire service.
'Come quickly,' he said
'There's a fire in Wellington Square!'

Chapter 2

'Stay Back!'

PC Kent ran across the road and raced through the gardens. The smoke was coming from behind Fred's shed.

As PC Kent arrived, a sheet of flames shot up, and the back wall of the shed was on fire.

'What if Brian is inside the shed?' cried Mr Keeping.

'I've got to save him!'

PC Kent grabbed him by the arm.
'Stay back!' he said. 'It isn't safe.
We must wait for the firefighters to come.'

Some people were starting to gather around.
'Stay back!' said PC Kent.

Bang! There was an explosion. The door blew out. Then bang! Another explosion. And bang! Another one.

Fred came running over. 'That will be the paint tins,' he said.

When they heard the explosions lots more people came to see what was going on.

PC Kent made them all stay back.

Flames were pouring out of the door and
windows of the shed.
Sparks were flying everywhere.

'If the firefighters don't get here soon,
the trees will catch light,' said Mrs Valentine.
'If the trees catch light, the fire could spread
to the houses.'

People were starting to panic.

PC Kent told everyone to keep calm.

'The fire engine will be here soon,' he said.

But the minutes were ticking by and the flames were getting bigger all the time.

Chapter 3

PC Kent Investigates

At last, they heard a siren, and then a fire engine arrived. The firefighters jumped out. They set up their hoses.
Soon, they had put the fire out.

As the smoke began to clear, everyone stood looking at what was left of Fred's shed. One of the firefighters found something in the ashes. He called PC Kent.

'I don't think it was an accident,' he said.

'It looks like someone set fire to the shed!'

PC Kent looked at the match pack.

'... llers Garage,' he read.

Miller's Garage ... Kevin Miller!

That boy was always getting into trouble!

PC Kent looked for some more clues.

He saw a glove…

Where had he seen a glove like that before?

He saw a dog's paw print... Max?
If Max had been here, you could be sure
Rocky wasn't very far away.

He saw some bits of paper... they were just
like the one Mr Patel had given him from
Jamila's notepad!

Then PC Kent noticed something else.
There were sweet papers all over the place.
He shook his head.
Those kids were in big trouble now!

Chapter 4

Big Touble!

PC Kent said, 'Is there anything you want
to tell me?'
Kevin, Tessa, Rocky and Jamila looked at
the ground.
None of them said a word.
'Perhaps I should talk to your parents then,'
said PC Kent.
Jamila looked up in horror. 'No! Please don't
tell my dad!'
'It was an accident!' said Rocky.
'We didn't mean to set fire to the shed,'
said Tessa.
Kevin didn't say anything.

PC Kent asked them to tell him what
had happened.

'Well, we had this big heap of sweet papers,'
Jamila said.

'And we thought we could burn them,
like Fred burns the leaves,' said Tessa.

'Kevin got some matches from his dad's garage,'
said Rocky.

'But we couldn't get the sweet papers to light,
so Jamila gave us some pages from her notepad.'

'We still couldn't get the bonfire to light,
so we left it and went to play on the swings.'

'Then we saw the smoke ...'

PC Kent said he could arrest them all for criminal damage. Tessa, Jamila and Rocky looked shocked.
But Kevin said, 'What's the big deal? It was only a shed!'

'Someone could have been hurt,' PC Kent said.
'The fire could have spread to the trees.
If Brian had been hiding in the shed,
he would have been killed.'
'I didn't think of that,' said Kevin.
'Well, next time, think before you act,'
said PC Kent.

Chapter 5

The Real Thief

'And another thing,' said PC Kent.
'Where did you get the sweet papers from?
A big box of sweets was stolen from Mr Patel's
shop this morning.'
'We didn't steal anything!' cried Jamila.
'We found the sweet papers,' said Tessa.

They showed PC Kent where they had found
the sweet papers.
Something floated down.

'Brian!' they exclaimed.

'There's my chimp,' cried Mr Keeping.

'And there's your thief!' said PC Kent to
Mr Patel.

Mr Keeping thanked PC Kent for coming to
Wellington Square.
'You caught a thief and found a missing chimp.
You found out who started the fire.
Then you talked to them so they won't
do it again.'

'It's all in a day's work!' said PC Kent.